CONTENTS

ALL ABOUT
Superhero
HARRY

NAME: Harrison Albert Cruz

FAVOURITE COLOUR: red

FAVOURITE FOOD: spaghetti

FAVOURITE SCHOOL SUBJECT: science

HOBBIES: playing video games, inventing and reading

IDOLS: Albert Einstein and Superman

BEST FRIEND, NEIGHBOUR, AND SIDEKICK: Macy

LATEST INVENTION: Super Roby

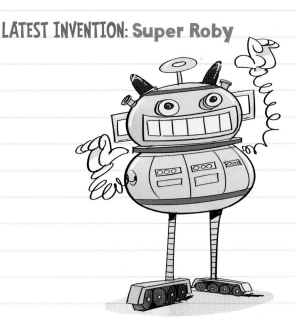

CHAPTER 1

CHORES! BLAH!

It's Saturday! Harry leaps out of bed. He has a full day planned.

After breakfast, he'll ride his bike to the park. This afternoon, his dad is taking him to see the new *Superman* movie. And after dinner, he'll work on his latest superhero invention.

Harry loves superheroes. He wishes he had real superpowers. But he doesn't, so he creates superhero inventions to make him more superhero-ish.

One time Harry made a super suctionator. It was supposed to pick up Harry's Lego bricks. Instead, it picked up the cat.

Another time Harry made a super tooth brusher. It was supposed to brush Harry's teeth for him. Instead, it squirted toothpaste in his eyes and tried to brush his eyebrows!

It seems like Harry fails at all of his attempts to be super. But Harry never stops trying.

"Harry!" his mum calls. "Before you go out, you have to finish your chores."

Oh, right. Chores. Harry had purposely forgotten about those. Harry quickly cleans his room and the big fish tank.

Before he heads for the door, Harry puts on his favourite blue superhero boots with the lightning bolts. They're a little too big on him, but he wears them anyway.

"Be back soon, Mum!" he calls.

"Harry, can you please take
the rubbish on your way out?"
Mum asks.

In his apartment building, the rubbish chute is at the end of the corridor.

As Harry runs down the hall, he trips over his boots. He drops the bag and spills rubbish everywhere. Split pea soup from last night's dinner splats all over his shirt, trousers, and his favourite boots.

Harry's had it with chores! He knows exactly what his next superhero invention is going to be, and it's going to be awesome.

CHAPTER 2

MEET SUPER ROBY

On Sunday Harry wakes up extra early to finish working on his latest invention.

It's a real live robot! Harry used his robot kit from his birthday to start it. Then he added a few of his own things to make the robot extra useful.

"Super Roby, you look awesome!" Harry says. "Now let's see if you work."

Harry dumps his basket of dirty clothes onto his bedroom floor.

"Here goes nothing!" Harry pushes some buttons on a remote control. Then he waits.

Super Roby starts picking up the clothes!

"Awesome!" Harry yells. "Now let's see if you can put the clothes into the basket."

Harry pushes more buttons.

Once again, Super Roby does
as he's commanded.

"Woo-hoo!" Harry shouts.

"Super Roby really works!"

"Amazing Macy to Superhero Harry. Come in, Superhero Harry. Over."

Macy is Harry's neighbour. She's also his superhero sidekick, classmate, and best friend. She lives across the courtyard.

"Copy that, Amazing Macy. Superhero Harry here. Over."

"Bad news. I can't come over to work on our super secret hideout today. Over," replies Macy.

"Why not? Over," Harry says.

"I have to reorganise the playroom. It's a mess! Over."

Harry says, "I don't have to worry about doing chores anymore. Over."

"What do you mean? Over," replies Macy.

"I invented a robot to do my chores for me. Over."

"Does it actually work? Over," asks Macy.

"You'll see for yourself tomorrow," Harry says. "I'm bringing him to the class science fair. Over and out!"

* * *

After breakfast, Harry's mum asks, "Can you please sweep the kitchen floor?"

"No problem, Mum!" Harry says. Then he puts Super Roby on the case.

Harry puts the broom in Roby's hands. Then he pushes some buttons on the remote control. *Shazam!*

Super Roby is sweeping the kitchen floor! Harry put his feet up while he reads a superhero comic book.

"This is the life," Harry says.

CHAPTER 3

SUPER ROBY RULES

"Okay, class," Ms Lane says. "It's time to present your science projects. When everyone is done we will vote, and I will announce the winner."

Violet goes first. She made a toy race car out of a plastic drinks bottle. She used bottle caps for wheels and a computer battery to make it run.

Ethan is next. He added a lift to his sister's dollhouse. He shows how it moves up and down with a remote control.

Then it's Macy's turn. She made magnetic superhero wrist cuffs. When she holds them up, Ms Lane's paper clips move her way.

It's finally Harry's turn. He wheels Roby to the front of the room.

"This is Super Roby. That's short for Superhero Robot," Harry says proudly.

"What does Super Roby do?" Melanie asks.

"What would you like him to do?" Harry asks.

"Can he throw away this broken pencil?" Melanie asks.

Harry puts the broken pencil in Super Roby's hand. He pushes some buttons on his remote.

Off Super Roby goes to throw away Melanie's pencil away. His robot actually works!

"Should Super Roby erase the white board?" Harry asks, picking up an eraser.

"Sure, Harry," Ms Lane says. "Or should I say, Super Roby."

"Now this I've got to see!" Violet says.

Harry places the eraser in Super Roby's grip. He pushes some buttons on his remote control. Super Roby moves the eraser back and forth across the board.

"Harry, I am super impressed," Ms Lane says. "Please tell us how you made your robot. How does he work?"

"It's simple, I just use this remote –"

That's when Harry's remote control starts making weird noises. The buttons light up, but Harry is not pushing them.

"Hey! Super Roby took my water bottle!" Serena shouts. "And he's heading out of the door!"

CHAPTER 4

ROBOT ON THE LOOSE

"Sorry, Serena! That wasn't supposed to happen," Harry says. "I'll get your water bottle back. After all, I'm Superhero Harry, and I will save the day!"

Then he asks, "Ms Lane, can I go chase my robot?"

"Please Harry, and hurry!" she says.

Once in the hallway, Harry doesn't see Super Roby anywhere. Then he hears someone shout.

"A robot just dropped a bottle of water in my lap!"

Harry runs in the direction of the voice. He reaches Mr Kent's classroom.

"Any chance you've seen a robot lately?" Harry asks.

"We certainly did," Mr Kent says. "He rolled in here and made a huge mess! His lights were blinking, and he was making loud noises."

"Do you know which direction he went? I have to stop him," Harry says.

"That way!" all the children shout. Harry takes off again.

"Help! That robot is trying to eat my chocolate chip cookies!" a kid exclaims.

Uh-oh! When Harry reaches Mr Stark's classroom, Super Roby is there. He's smashing chocolate chip cookies against his head! He's making a big mess!

"Who is responsible for this runaway robot?" Mr Stark asks.

"I am, sir, but I can't seem to stop him," Harry says. "The remote control just went crazy. Wait, where is the remote control?"

"Harry, there you are!" Macy says, running into Mr Stark's classroom. "I have your remote!"

"Your robot is pulling papers out of our drawers," a boy says.

Papers are flying everywhere.

"What am I going to do, Macy? Harry asks.

"You made Super Roby, and you can fix him," Macy says.

"You're right," Harry says.

"Just think about how you built him," Macy says. "And then go backwards."

"Your robot just left," Mr Stark says. He looks really annoyed.

"Don't worry," Harry says. "I know how to stop him!"

CHAPTER 5

EVEN SUPERHEROES DO CHORES

Harry and Macy race back to their classroom. Super Roby is there too, and he's causing more chaos.

"Your robot just scribbled all over my work!" a girl shouts.

"I'm really sorry. But I think I figured out how to stop him," Harry says. "Macy, hold him in place."

"He's a little out of control," Macy says. "I may need some help."

"Right," Harry says. "Macy, can you hold his hands? Ms Lane, can you hold him in place?"

"Happy to help, Harry," Ms Lane says.

Macy grabs the robot's hands. Ms Lane grabs his body. Harry tinkers with some wires.

"I created Super Roby to do my chores," Harry says. "This is the wire that makes him do that. It must have shorted out."

"Less talking and more working,"
Ms Lane says. "We can't hold him
forever."

Harry pulls out the wire. Super
Roby stops moving.

Harry and Macy high five.

Ms Lane shakes her head.

"See Superhero Harry? You did save the day!" Macy says.

"Harry Cruz, please come to the headteacher's office," says a voice from the loudspeaker. "Calling Harry Cruz."

It's Mrs Banner.

"Go ahead, Harry," Ms Lane says.

Harry drags his feet all the way to Mrs Banner's office. This is not how the day was supposed to go.

Harry's parents are already
with Mrs Banner. That is not a
good sign.

"Harry, you caused quite a bit
of trouble with your robot today,"
Mrs Banner says.

"Harry, what happened?"
his dad asks.

"I don't like chores. I made
Super Roby so he would do my
chores for me," Harry says.

"Harry, nobody likes doing
chores," his mum says. "But it's
something we all have to do.
Even parents do chores."

"Superheroes don't have to do
chores!" Harry says.

"Of course they do, Harry,"
Mrs Banner says.

"They do?" Harry asks.

"Think about it," she says. "Do superheroes use their superpowers to vacuum, fold laundry or do other things they can easily do themselves?"

"No, I guess not," Harry says.

"They use their powers for more important things," Mrs Banner says. "Like helping people in need."

"I'm really sorry for all the trouble Super Roby and I caused today," Harry says. "And now I know a better way to use Super Roby."

"And what is that?" his mum asks.

"We are going to help grandma clean her house," Harry says.

"That's a great idea, Harry!" his dad says.

"Let's get going!" Harry says.

"Superhero Harry, over and out!"

GLOSSARY

attempts tries to complete something

chaos complete confusion

chute narrow tube or passage

commanded gave an order

courtyard open space that is surrounded completely or partly by a building or group of buildings

impressed feel respect for someone or something

invention useful new device

magnetic relating to a magnet, which is a piece of material that is able to attract certain metals

reorganise organise something again

sidekick person who helps and spends a lot of time with someone

tinker try to repair something

TALK ABOUT IT

1. Do you think science fairs are important? Why or why not?

2. Do you think it's important to do chores? Explain your anwer.

3. Do you think Harry should have gotten in trouble for the mess his robot caused? Why or why not?

WRITE ABOUT IT

1. Write a paragraph about an invention or project you would make for a science fair.

2. Make a list of chores you do at home. Put them in order from easiest to hardest.

3. Pretend you are the headteacher. Write a paragraph describing what you would have done with Harry and his robot.

ABOUT THE
AUTHOR

Rachel Ruiz is the author of several children's books. She was inspired to write her first picture book, When Penny met POTUS, after working for Barack Obama on his re-election campaign in 2012.

When Rachel isn't writing books, she writes and produces TV shows and documentaries. She lives in Chicago, Illinois, USA, with her husband and their daughter.

ABOUT THE ILLUSTRATOR

Steve May is a professional illustrator and animation director. He says he spent his childhood drawing lots of things and discovering interesting ways of injuring himself.

Steve's work has become a regular feature in the world of children's books. He still draws lots but injures himself less regularly now. He lives in glamourous north London, and his mum says he's a genius.

BE A **SUPERHERO** AND READ THEM ALL!

The Superhero Project

by Rachel Ruiz Illustrated by Steve May

The Runaway Robot

by Rachel Ruiz Illustrated by Steve May

The Wild Field Trip

by Rachel Ruiz Illustrated by Steve May

The Breaktime Bully

by Rachel Ruiz Illustrated by Steve May